# It's Not Worth Making a Tzimmes Over!

**Betsy R. Rosenthal**

Illustrated by **Ruth Rivers**

Albert Whitman & Company, Morton Grove, Illinois

For my mom, the hippest grandma around, my dad, who taught me to love words, and to Sonya and Ann, for sharing your talents with me.—B.R.R.

For Gus and Archie.—R.R.

Library of Congress Cataloging-in-Publication Data

Rosenthal, Betsy R.
It's not worth making a tzimmes over! / by Betsy Rosenthal ; illustrated by Ruth Rivers.
p. cm.
Summary: Sara and her grandma add too much yeast to the challah dough and it grows so big that it threatens to take over the whole neighborhood. Includes a glossary of Yiddish words.
ISBN-13 978-0-8075-3677-3 (hardcover)
ISBN-10 0-8075-3677-6 (hardcover)
[1. Grandmothers—Fiction. 2. Challah (Bread)—Fiction. 3. Bread—Fiction. 4. Baking—Fiction. 5. Jews—United States—Fiction. 6. Humorous stories.] I. Title: It is not worth making a tzimmes over. II. Rivers, Ruth, ill. III. Title.
PZ7.R7194453Its 2006 [E]—dc22 2005024624

The design is by Carol Gildar.

For more information about Albert Whitman & Company, visit our web site at www.albertwhitman.com.

One Friday morning during summer vacation, Grandma said, "Let's make a challah, bubbela."

My name is Sara, but she calls everyone bubbela.

"Sure, Grandma, what do we need?" I asked.

"Oh, a bisel of this and a bisel of that," she said.

With one hand Grandma cracked some eggs into a glass and stirred them up. Then she set out some yeast and a bunch of other ingredients on the table, along with a glass of orange juice and a bagel for me.

YEAST

"Let's get started," Grandma said. "Now, where's that flour?"
While she rummaged through the cupboard looking for it,
I poured the water and honey into the bowl.
"Don't forget to add the yeast," she called out.
"Did it already, Grandma."
"Now shayna maydala, we mix in the oil and the eggs."

I took the glass next to me and poured the yellow goop into the bowl. I poured the oil, too, and mixed it around like Grandma told me.

"Oy, bubbela, you poured your orange juice into the challah mix!"

"Oops, sorry."

"It's not worth making a tzimmes over," she said. "How about I'll add the eggs and you add the flour."

I poured in the flour and my jeans turned white.

"Mix it up well, then I'll show you how to knead the dough."

My hands looked like a duck's webbed feet with all that dough stuck between my fingers. I added more flour like Grandma said, and this time I turned her gray hair white.

"Oops!" I exclaimed. "Sorry about that."

"It's not worth making a tzimmes over," she said. "Put the dough in the bowl to rise, and we'll come back later for the next step."

She laid a towel over the bowl and said, "Come on, let's play a little badminton."

"Oy," I said to myself and followed her outside.

The first time she served to me, the birdie bounced off my head.

"Got a hole in your racket, bubbela?" Grandma asked me.

"Can we stop now and watch a movie?" I asked Grandma after the birdie whacked me in the nose for the third time.

We flipped through the 988 channels and finally found an old horror movie. "*The Blob!* One of my absolute favorites!" Grandma said. "Oh, I love that scene at the theater when the Blob eats the projectionist!"

Grandma and I were sprawled out on the couch, watching, when I felt it—something gooey was wrapping itself around my feet.

"Aaaahh," I shouted. "It's the Blob!"

"Vay iz mir, it's everywhere!" Grandma cried as she looked around the room.

"It's coming from the kitchen!" I yelled.

"It's the challah!" she screamed. "We forgot all about it!"

We yanked our feet out of the dough and ran
next door to Mrs. DeLuca's house, dough oozing at our
heels. By the time we got there, the dough had covered
Grandma's front lawn and was spreading down the street.

"May we use your phone, Liz?" Grandma asked frantically.

"Be my guest," Mrs. DeLuca answered. "I'm watching
*The Blob* in the other room."

Grandma called the police. "Please come over to 2155 Crestview Drive right away! My challah dough has taken over the house, and it's headed down the street."

"Are they coming, Grandma?" I asked when she hung up.

"You know what that meshuggina policeman said? He said, 'Thanks for letting us know, lady. Call us back if it starts jaywalking.'"

"Oh, it's all my fault, Grandma. If I hadn't added the orange juice…"

She looked at me with her eyebrows squeezed together. "Never mind about the orange juice, bubbela. How much yeast did you put in that bowl?"

"I just used all the packets in the box you left on the table."

"Oy veh! There were fifty-six packets in that box. We only needed two!"

"Sorry, Grandma."

"It's not worth making a tzimmes over," she said.

"Grandma, are we still going to bake the challah?" I was trying to imagine how we could fit all that dough in Grandma's oven.

"Of course we are, shayna maydala."

We looked outside Mrs. DeLuca's house. The challah dough had taken over Crestview Drive and was heading west on Willowbrook Lane. I had an idea and I shared it with Grandma.

"It's a good one!" Grandma said. "What sechel you have, bubbela!"

"Mrs. DeLuca," I called, "may we borrow your computer?"

"Help yourself, dear," she called back, still glued to the TV.

Together, Grandma and I figured out what to write. We printed copy after copy.

We took off on Grandma's motor scooter,
and I stuck a flyer on every doorstep we passed.

We saw the challah dough seeping around the corner of Willowbrook Lane at Durant.

Riding back to Grandma's house, we noticed whole chunks of the challah were missing. Scrumptious baking smells followed us all the way home.

We forced the front door open and waded our way into the kitchen. Gathering up as much challah dough as we could, we braided some and twisted some and shoved it all into the oven to bake.

We were cleaning the dough off the floor when
we heard pounding on the front door.
"POLICE—OPEN UP!"

"All right, all right, I'm coming," Grandma said as she opened the door. A big burly officer barged in and held up our flyer:

Dear Neighbors,
Look outside and help yourself—
there's challah dough for everyone.
Bake it till it's golden brown,
and then you'll know the challah's done.
Sara Strauss and Grandma Strauss

"Ma'am, are you responsible for this dough attack on the neighborhood?" the policeman asked Grandma.

Grandma put her hands on her hips. "And are you the police officer who refused to send help when I called about the challah dough on the loose? You didn't think it was worth making a tzimmes over, did you?"

"Well, uh . . . " the officer sniffed the air. "What *is* that wonderful smell?"

He followed Grandma into the kitchen. She pulled a humongous challah out of the oven, blew on it a little, then tore off a piece and popped it into the officer's mouth.

"Would you like some jam to go with that?" I asked him.

"And maybe a little tea?" Grandma added. "Sit down, sit down," she said to him.

"Mmm, that's why the whole neighborhood smells so good," he said in between bites.

"Take a flyer home," I said to the officer as he left. "It's got the recipe on the back."

"Sorry again that I put so much yeast in the mix," I told Grandma.

"Never mind—the whole neighborhood got to share our challah. Anyway, I was the one who caused all the tsuris, bubbela. I should've told you how much yeast to put in."

Just then, Mom came to pick me up. "My gosh, what happened here?" she asked.

Grandma and I winked at each other. "Oh," we both said, "nothing worth making a tzimmes over!"

# Challah a l'Orange

*Ingredients*

1 ½ cups warm water
½ cup honey
only 2 packages
   rapid-rise yeast!
1 ½ tsp. salt
⅓ cup vegetable oil
½ cup orange juice

2 eggs
4 egg yolks plus
   2 more egg yolks
6 cups (plus some extra) flour
1 Tbsp. sugar
raisins (optional)
poppy seeds
vegetable shortening
   (for greasing the pan)

In a large bowl, combine water, honey, yeast, and salt. Stir until yeast dissolves. Mix in oil, orange juice, eggs, and 4 egg yolks. Add 6 cups flour and mix to form soft dough.

Knead on a lightly floured surface for about 8 minutes (it's good exercise), until dough is smooth and elastic. Add more flour sparingly as needed to the surface and/or your hands. Add raisins by pressing them into the dough with your fingers.

Place in a floured bowl, cover, and let rise for 25 minutes (while you play a little badminton).

Divide dough in half. Divide each half into 3 pieces. Squeeze each piece out into a 10-inch rope. Braid the 3 ropes to form challah, pinching ends together. Repeat with other half. To make a round loaf, roll dough into a 30-inch rope. Holding one end, wind the rest into a spiral that's a little higher in the center. Place each challah on a cookie sheet greased lightly with vegetable shortening.

Combine sugar and remaining 2 egg yolks in a small bowl. Using a pastry brush, brush each challah with egg mixture. Lightly sprinkle poppy seeds on top. Let rest for 20 minutes.

Bake at 400 degrees for 15 minutes; reduce temperature to 350 and bake for 20 minutes more. Loaves should be golden brown.

Let cool, then don't make a tzimmes over it— just eat it!

# Some Yiddish Words

Yiddish is the historical language of the Jews of Central and Eastern Europe. Although it is no longer spoken fluently by most Jews in the world, many Yiddish words, like *bagel* and *klutz*, have seeped into the English language. Yiddish is a language so rich in humor and flavor that even non-Jewish people enjoy using its words.

**bisel** (BIS-ul): a little.

**bubbela** (BUB-eh-luh): endearing way to address friends, children, and other loved ones. The word means "little grandmother."

**challah** (KHAH-luh): (for the "kh," make a rattling sound as though you're clearing your throat). A braided or round egg bread, used particularly on the Sabbath and Jewish holidays.

**meshuggina** (muh-SHOOG-in-uh): crazy, absurd.

**oy!** or **oy veh!** (oy VAY): oh, no!

**sechel** (SAY-khul): (for the "kh," make a rattling sound as though you're clearing your throat). Common sense, smarts.

**shayna maydala** (SHAY-nuh MAY-duh-luh): beautiful girl.

**tsuris** (TSOO-riss): trouble.

**tzimmes** (TSIM-mess): a fuss, a big deal; also refers to a stew of carrots, prunes, sweet potatoes, and other vegetables.

**vay iz mir** (VAY iz meer): woe is me!